TINY'S
BATH

For M. and D.
—C. M.

To my ninety-five-year-old grandmother,
Gaga, who showed me how to love laughter,
a good story, and God. I love you.
—R. D.

PUFFIN BOOKS
Published by the Penguin Group
Penguin Putnam Inc., 375 Hudson Street, New York, New York 10014, U.S.A.
Penguin Books Ltd, 27 Wrights Lane, London W8 5TZ, England
Penguin Books Australia Ltd, Ringwood, Victoria, Australia
Penguin Books Canada Ltd, 10 Alcorn Avenue, Toronto, Ontario, Canada M4V 3B2
Penguin Books (N.Z.) Ltd, 182-190 Wairau Road, Auckland 10, New Zealand

Penguin Books Ltd, Registered Offices: Harmondsworth, Middlesex, England

First published by Puffin Books and Viking, members of Penguin Putnam Books for
Young Readers, 1999

5   7   9   10   8   6   4

LIBRARY OF CONGRESS CATALOGING-IN-PUBLICATION DATA
Meister, Cari.
Tiny's bath / by Cari Meister ; illustrated by Rich Davis.   p. cm.
Summary: Tiny is a very big dog who loves to dig, and when it is time for his bath,
his owner has trouble finding a place to bathe him.
ISBN 0-670-87962-2 (Viking : hc).—ISBN 0-14-130267-4 (Puffin : pb)
[1. Dogs—Fiction. 2. Baths—Fiction.] I. Davis, Rich, date, ill. II. Title.
PZ7.M515916Ti 1998 [E]—dc21 98-3844 CIP AC
Printed in U.S.A.
Puffin® and Easy-to-Read® are registered trademarks of Penguin Putnam Inc.

Reading level 1.3

TINY'S
BATH

by Cari Meister
illustrated by Rich Davis

PUFFIN BOOKS

I have a very large dog.

His name is Tiny.

He is bigger than a bike.

He is bigger than a chair.

He is bigger than I am!

Tiny likes to dig.

He is dirty.

He needs a bath.

The pail is too small.

The sink is too small.

The bathtub is too small.

Where can I give Tiny a bath?

My pool!

Get the hose.

Get the brush. Get the soap.

Scrub, scrub, scrub.

Oh no! Watch out!

Tiny is clean. I am wet.

Stop, Tiny! Come back!

Oh no! Mud!

Tiny is dirty.

I am dirty.

Back to the pool.

Good dog, Tiny.

Go, Tiny, go!

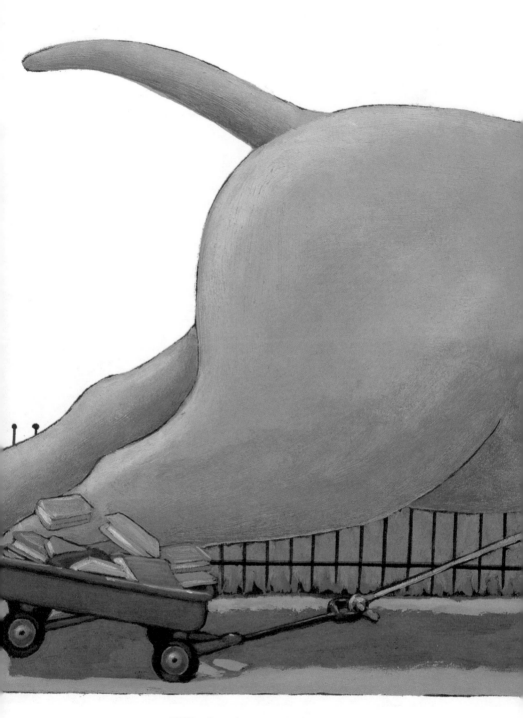

Wait for me!

Stop, Tiny, stop!

Tiny can!

I cannot pull the wagon.

Oh no! Too many books!

Tiny helps.

I fill the wagon.

I get bird books for Tiny.

I get dog books.

I get frog books.

Tiny stays outside.

I go inside.

You wait here.

No dogs in the library.

Sorry, Tiny.

Time to go!

I get my library card.

I get my wagon.

Today we are going to the library.

If I go to the lake, Tiny comes, too.

If I go to the park, Tiny comes, too.

He goes where I go.

He is my best friend.

This is Tiny.

TINY
GOES TO THE LIBRARY

For Judy, the best editor
in the whole wide world.
—C.M.

To Angie, my wife and best friend:
I'm so glad God brought us together
to make a home. I love you!
—R.D.

PUFFIN BOOKS
Published by the Penguin Group
Penguin Putnam Inc., 345 Hudson Street, New York, New York 10014, U.S.A.
Penguin Books Ltd, 27 Wrights Lane, London W8 5TZ, England

Penguin Books Ltd, Registered Offices: Harmondsworth, Middlesex, England

First published by Puffin Books and Viking,
divisions of Penguin Putnam Books for Young Readers, 2000

3 5 7 9 10 8 6 4

Text copyright © Cari Meister, 2000
Illustrations copyright © Rich Davis, 2000
All rights reserved

LIBRARY OF CONGRESS CATALOGING-IN-PUBLICATION DATA
Meister, Cari.
Tiny goes to the library / by Cari Meister : illustrated by Rich Davis.
p. cm. — (A Viking easy-to-read)
Summary: Tiny the dog is a big help at the library when his owner takes out too
many books to carry home.
ISBN 0-670-88556-8 (hc) — ISBN 0-14-130488-X (pbk)
[I. Libraries—Fiction 2. Books and reading—Fiction. 3. Dogs—Fiction.] I. Davis,
Rich, date– ill. II. Title. III. Series.
PZ7.M515916 Tg 2000 [E]—dc21 98-051134

Printed in U.S.A.

Reading level 1.3

TINY
GOES TO THE LIBRARY

by
Cari Meister

illustrated by
Rich Davis

PUFFIN BOOKS